A Kind of Magic

by

Catherine MacPhail

First published in 2001 in Great Britain by
Barrington Stoke Ltd, Sandeman House, Trunk's Close,
55 High St, Edinburgh EH1 1SR
www.barringtonstoke.co.uk

This edition published 2005

ISBN 1-842993-43-7

Printed in Great Britain by Bell & Bain Ltd

A Note from the Author

Britain has a wonderful history of magic stones. I am a bit like Nick in this story - I am willing to believe anything but I'm never quite sure. Maybe there is a logical explanation for every strange event.

Do you think what happened to Nick was really magic? I hope it was. It would be a far less exciting world if there wasn't some kind of magic in it.

Contents

Chapter 1
Finding the Fossil

"This is the most boring school trip I've ever been on," I moaned to my friend Ravi for the third time. "Why on earth are we searching on an empty beach for stones of all things? I still can't believe I'm here. Maybe I've died and gone to hell."

Ravi just looked at me and said, "I wish you'd do just that, Nick Black. Drop dead. Then maybe you'd shut up for a while."
He picked up yet another stone. "I think this is a brilliant day out."

"That's because you collect stones, Ravi," I told him. "You are the saddest guy I've ever come across."

"Thank you for your kind words," replied Ravi with a sarcastic shrug.

I went on moaning. "I mean, why couldn't we go looking for something interesting ... like creatures from another planet?"

Ravi shook his head and sneered. "Get real, Nick Black. Alien creatures land in deserts in America, not in Scottish towns like this. Nothing weird or wonderful ever happens here."

Just then I let out a yell. I had just kicked one of those grotty stones and a sharp pain shot up my leg. Ravi picked up the stone while I jumped about in agony, holding my foot and trying not to use bad language. He studied it very carefully, turning it in his hand.

"This is really something special," he said at last in an excited voice.

I stared at the stone and tried to pretend I was interested. "It's just another stone, Ravi."

"It's a very interesting stone," he told me.

He shouted over to our Geography teacher, Mr Dunn, or Goofy as we fondly called him.

Somewhere along the line Goofy had swapped his face with a racehorse. I'm sure of it. He looked even more like a racehorse when he laughed. He even sounded like a horse and when he was excited he laughed a lot.

Goofy grew very excited as he examined Ravi's stone. "This is not just a stone, Ravi," he said, "this is a fossil. Look here." He pointed out a funny shape in the stone. "Some strange creature from long ago has been trapped in there for millions of years. Oh, what a find! What a find!"

Goofy gathered the class around him. "Some of the very old Celtic tribes believed fossils like this had magic powers. They were thought to be very lucky."

"Not so lucky for the poor sod that got trapped inside it," I pointed out.

Everybody laughed but Goofy. Stones were a serious business with him.

I looked harder at the stone. "It's an ugly old creature in there," I told him, trying to sound interested.

"Must be a distant relative of yours then, Nick," Pamela replied.

I turned to find Pamela standing beside me. Now, I fancy Pamela like mad. And she knows it. My face always goes bright red when I see her and I can't seem to talk sense.

"I wish you'd stop playing hard to get, Pamela," I managed to blurt out, trying to sound cool. She just laughed at me and walked off with that amazing little wiggle of hers.

"For you, I'm not *hard* to get, Nick. I'm *impossible* to get." She giggled and all her friends giggled too. I went an even brighter shade of red.

Meanwhile, Goofy had handed Ravi's special stone back to him.

"Poor Goofy," Ravi whispered as we watched him walk away, his shoulders slumped. "I wish he could find an interesting stone."

"He's spoiled for choice here, son," I pointed down the length of the rocky beach. "Stones everywhere."

"No," Ravi explained, as if he was talking to an idiot. "I mean a special stone, like mine."

And that's exactly when things began to happen. Goofy started yelling and laughing and snorting like a horse. He held something up for us all to see. "Look! Look what I've found!"

It was a stone. Just a stone. Everyone gathered round him to admire his find.

Everyone but me.

I thought it was strange that, at the very moment that Ravi had wished for Goofy to find an interesting stone, Goofy picked up just the stone he was looking for. Oh, I know, everyone says I'd believe anything. Just like him in the *X-Files*. But hadn't Goofy told us that the old Celtic tribes believed some stones were magic? Could this stone be magic?

Goofy was desperate to find another fossil. "Let's give it another hour," he shouted.

"Another hour?" I yelled back. "This is worse than detention."

"Oh shut up," Ravi told me. "I think this is my lucky day. I feel I might just find something else."

And Ravi did.

Half an hour later he picked up a gold watch.

"That watch is worth a lot of money," I said. I was green with envy now. I hadn't found a thing, except an empty tube of toothpaste.

"Indeed it is." Goofy patted Ravi on the head. "I'm sure there will be a reward for a gold watch like that."

Ravi was smiling from ear to ear. This really was his lucky day. He had found a gold watch and now he had a reward to look forward to.

I hadn't found a thing. I admit that I hadn't been looking, but let's face it. Who wants to spend an afternoon looking for stones?

I began to think. It wasn't Ravi who had found that fossil stone. *I* had been the one to kick it with my foot. In fact, it was almost as if the stone had attacked me. Ravi had only picked it up. I was the one who had found it. By law, it was *my* fossil. Anyway, he was going to get a reward for that gold watch. Why should I go home empty-handed?

So I slipped my hand into his bag when he wasn't looking, took the stone and slipped it into my pocket.

Chapter 2
First Wish

Ravi didn't even notice the stone was missing. Not at the time. He had so many stones in his bag, one going missing didn't make any difference.

I slept with the stone under my pillow. I gripped it in my hand. It felt warm to the touch and my dreams that night were strange. I dreamt I was somewhere in the middle of a forest a long, long time ago. I was surrounded by a tribe, their faces covered in paint. They were chanting and dancing round a fire. They didn't notice me as I moved amongst them. I seemed to be invisible. Then I saw that they were passing a fossil stone, *my* stone, from one hand to another.

"Make a wish," I heard them chant. "What you wish for is what it shall be."

Then, all at once, they turned to me. They stared at me with wild eyes. Their faces glowed golden in the firelight and their chant became a tribal cry.

"What you wish for is what it shall be!"

And, suddenly, I was holding the stone and it seemed to be on fire. It was alive in the palm of my hand. I could almost see the long-dead creature wriggling and moving and ...

AAAGH!

I jumped awake. The dream was so real, I woke up sweating.

I was still gripping the stone in my hand.

Anything I wish for...? Could that really be true? There was only one way to find out.

It's not as easy to make a wish as you might think. I didn't want to waste it. What if I was only allowed one? What could I wish for? I decided not to be in too much of a hurry. I would wait a bit.

Later that day in class, Ravi was moaning on to old Goofy about his lost stone. "I don't know what happened to it, Mr Dunn. I only noticed it was missing this morning."

All the time they were talking, I was holding it tightly in my pocket. I hoped they didn't notice how red my face was.

Goofy was very understanding. "Never mind, Ravi. You did get a £50 reward for the gold watch."

A £50 reward, I thought. How lucky can you get?

Goofy shook his head. "I know, Ravi. You would much rather have the stone."

Ravi nodded. "Yes, I would, Sir."

And I think he meant it. The boy's mad.

We heard a sudden giggle from the corridor outside. We could all see our French teacher laughing with the deputy headmaster. She is gorgeous and we've discovered that she is called Anne-Marie. She looks exactly what a French bird should look like. Fantastic body and lovely, long legs. Half the school's in love with her. There was a long sigh. It was from Goofy. He was in love with her too. He was looking at her in just the same way he looked at his beloved stones.

He wandered away with his face drooping even more than usual.

"Poor old Goofy," Ravi said, watching him. "He doesn't stand a chance with our Anne-Marie.

If she can only wait till I'm 21, she can have me."

I gave Ravi a push. "We all fancy her, Ravi. Get in line behind the rest of the school," I told him.

Just then I had an idea. Maybe I could wish for Anne-Marie to fancy *me*.

While I was thinking this over, who should walk right past me and start to admire herself in the glass door?

Pamela.

No. Forget Anne-Marie. There was only one woman for me.

Pamela.

I made up my mind that this was going to be her lucky day.

It took all my courage to go up to her. She was brushing her golden red hair and smiling at herself in the glass. I watched her

for a long time without saying anything.
She just ignored me. But then, she always
ignored me. At last I found the nerve to talk
to her. "You should wear purple lipstick,
Pamela. I think it would really suit you."

Her lips were much her best feature.
She had these soft, full lips and I just longed
to kiss them. I know this sounds sad, but I
couldn't help it.

She turned to me very slowly and glared
at me. "Like to lend me yours then?" she
said.

I don't know why she always has to insult
me. I only try to be nice to her.

However, I said nothing. I just thought to
myself, soon Pamela will be throwing herself
at me.

"How would you like to fall madly in love
with me, Pamela?" I asked her.

She hesitated, but only for a moment.
Then she began to laugh. She laughed so
loudly that everyone turned to watch us.
She must have laughed for a full minute.
Then she stopped. She drew in her breath
and she glared at me again. "Fall madly in
love with you, Nick Black? I'd rather have
zits."

Then she wiggled off, gathering up her
giggling friends. She clattered down the
corridor to her next class.

I have never been so shamed in all my life.
Everyone was watching me. Everyone was
laughing at me.

I had never insulted this girl – well, not
often anyway – and here she was going out of
her way to be cruel to me. You can only take
so many insults. Pamela had insulted me
once too often.

My fingers closed round the fossil in my pocket. If I wanted, I could wish for Pamela to come running back to me, right now, for her to fall on her knees and kiss my feet.

But no, wait a moment.

I could wish for something much better than that.

Something Pamela had told me she would rather have.

Zits.

Chapter 3
Zits!

Pamela didn't appear at school all the next morning. She didn't arrive till after dinner. That was just as well, because with a face like hers she would have put everybody off their food.

I have never seen so many zits. Her face looked like the surface of the moon. Her eyes had almost vanished and her nose just looked like another huge zit.

"What on earth happened to your face, Pamela?" one of her friends called out to her.

Pamela was almost in tears. "Don't ask me. You know I have lovely skin. I always take such good care of it. But I used a new face cream last night and I woke up this morning looking like this."

"Why on earth did you come to school?" someone else asked. "With a face like that I would have stayed at home."

Pamela pointed her zits at this so-called friend. "I didn't want to come. My Mum made me."

I gave the whole class time to come up close to her and inspect her disgusting zits. Then I walked slowly over to her and said my bit. "Just think, Pamela. Only yesterday you said you'd prefer zits to me. And now, you've got your wish. Is that strange, or what?"

There was a long pause. Pamela just stared at me. "What do you mean by that, Nick Black?"

I shrugged my shoulders. "I'm just saying. You wished for zits and you got them."

I'm sure at that point her zits began to quiver.

"Maybe," I went on, "if you'd been nicer to me you wouldn't be so ugly today."

Pamela was not going to say she was sorry. Even with a face full of zits she refused to be humble.

She gave me a sarcastic smile. "Yes, Nick, but my zits will be gone soon and I'll look gorgeous again. Whereas *you* will always be ugly."

I didn't even bother to get angry with her. "It will take them a couple of days to go," I told her, "so meanwhile, just to show I don't hold any bad feelings, I thought I'd give you something to hide them."

And I handed her a brown paper bag. "Do us all a favour. Wear that over your head for the next couple of days."

Everyone in the class started to laugh loudly. This time the joke was on Pamela. She thought she was above most of them because she was so pretty, so no-one felt the least bit sorry for her now.

While we all laughed she just stood there, boiling with anger. "I'd like to thank you for being so thoughtful," she said at last. "You've always wanted to kiss me, Nick. Now your wish is going to come true."

And with that, she grabbed me by the ears and dragged me towards her.

I had longed to kiss Pamela. It was the stuff of dreams.

But this was a nightmare. All I could see was a heaving surface of green and yellow zits hurtling closer to my face. I'm sure as she hit me several burst on impact. I tried to pull away from her, but Pamela is a strong girl. And she wasn't so much kissing me, as rubbing her zits all over my face. Some of them had come to a head and were scratching my cheeks. I began to feel really sick.

The class were going wild. Some of them were turning as green as Pamela's zits. They were clapping. They were groaning. Some had to run from the classroom to be sick.

The only thing that saved me was Anne-Marie rushing in and screaming, "What is going on here?"

At last, Pamela let go of my ears. She was grinning from zit to zit.

Now it was my turn to be sick.

I felt ill all day just thinking about it and when I got home I spent hours scrubbing my face in the bathroom. Then I went straight to bed. I did not come out of my room till the next morning.

"Are you OK, Nick?" my Mum asked me as she handed a sandwich through the door. "Your face looks funny."

Her face would look funny too if it had been through what mine had.

By morning, it wasn't just my face that was looking funny.

By morning my whole body, from head to toe, was covered in big, bulging zits.

I couldn't even sit down at the breakfast table. I was scared I would burst the zits on my backside. Yes, they were there too.
"I don't think I can go to school," I said weakly.

My Mum was having none of that. "You'll go to school, my boy!" She was pushing me out the door. "You've got your exams coming up soon and this time you've got to do better."

Pamela. Pamela and her kissing had done this. Surely no-one would have blamed me if I'd murdered her when I got to school.

Hers was the first laugh I heard as I limped into Goofy's class. "Oh look, we're twins," she shouted.

Everybody looked then and thought it was madly funny.

Goofy at least tried to make me feel better. "Don't worry, Nick. Most boys your age get spots. I did."

I tried to smile to show I was grateful but it was too painful.

Then he added, "They'll be gone in a couple of years."

A couple of years!

As I eased myself down onto my seat someone made a squelching sound. It was Pamela.

"I'm going home," I told Ravi at lunchtime. "I'm going to the doctor and I'll get a sick note."

"No. You will not!" A voice boomed behind me. It was Mr Gordon, our football coach. We called him Big Gordy. "Have you forgotten you're in the team for the semi-final tomorrow? We shall need every player we've got."

I pointed out, in case he hadn't noticed, that I was covered in zits. "I can't play like this, Mr Gordon."

"I don't care if your head's been cut off. As long as you've got two legs you're going to play. Now you be here for that match, or I'll come and drag you here."

Chapter 4
Football Fever

Next day I tried again. "I can't go out on the football pitch looking like this!" I protested to Big Gordy. But did he listen?

"I admit you look like a zit on legs. A zit that is ready to burst," Big Gordy said and looked at me as if he was about to vomit. "But go out there you will. And you'll play your best. This is the semi-final."

He gave me a push that sent me flying through the dressing room door and a couple more zits exploded as he did it. It didn't help that our strip was green and yellow. Yes, exactly the same colour as the zits. You couldn't tell where the strip ended and the zits began.

Of course, the first person I saw, or rather heard, as I ran onto the pitch, was Pamela. She was standing on the touchline laughing like a hyena. The whole crowd was finding the sight of me either wildly funny, or just plain sick-making.

"He shouldn't be allowed out in public!" I heard a woman say. I've got a funny feeling she was talking to my mother.

"He's making me feel sick," someone else said as I passed.

"Don't be silly," said another voice. "That's the funniest sight I've seen in years."

Now, how is a player supposed to give of his best with all this happening around him?

Well, I decided, I'd show them. Zits or no zits, I was going to win this match for the team.

I threw myself into tackle after tackle.

I went for the ball every time I had a chance.

It turned out to be much easier than I thought it was going to be.

At half-time I understood why I got the ball so often. Big Gordy told me.

"The other team are terrified to come near you," he said, slapping me on the back. Squelch went another few zits. "You are so disgusting."

I think he meant it as a compliment.

It was true. I was the hero of the match. Whenever I got the ball I had a free run to the goal. Not one of the other team had the courage to tackle me, to bring me down.

We won 3-0 thanks to me. I scored all three goals. And did my team rush over to hug me? Did they lift me high on their shoulders?

No. All I got from them after every score was a long distance wave.

At the final whistle the crowd went wild. Even Pamela was jumping up and down with delight.

"We're in the Final! We're in the Final," she yelled.

Then the whole school took up her words and chanted them at the tops of their voices. The team sprinted back to the dressing rooms. They were all being slapped on the back.

All of them, except me.

At least, I thought, in the dressing rooms I would be heaped with praise and thanks. But I was wrong again. This should have been my finest hour. But I might as well not have been there. No-one would even sit beside me on the bench.

They were all talking about the Final. But no-one was talking to me. I lifted my towel and stood up to go into the showers. Robbo, the captain of the team, held me back. I noticed his hand on my shoulder was protected by a towel.

"Sorry, Nick." He at least had the decency to look embarrassed. "But me and the boys have been talking and we've decided we're not going into the showers with you. You can wait. Go in after us."

I was really angry now. "This is crazy. I played a great game. I scored all the goals. And this is the thanks I get."

One of the other boys shouted across to me. "Can you blame us? We could all catch your zits. I mean, you got them off Pamela."

"Don't worry, I'm not going to kiss you!" I shouted back.

"You're not coming in the shower with us either, pal."

So, I was left sitting on the bench while the rest of the team laughed and sang and celebrated and had a good time in the showers. I could hear them joking about me.

To say I was angry was putting it mildly.

I was *furious*.

Big Gordy came in with his after-the-match treat. Hot dogs from Joe's Hot Dog Stand. Or Greasy Joe as we fondly call him. Big Gordy was carrying a huge box of hot dogs.

"Not in the showers yet?" he asked me.

"They wouldn't let me in with them," I moaned.

He nodded as if he understood. "Never mind, son. You and your zits played a brilliant game today." He threw not one, but two hot dogs at me. "Here. That's your treat for being man of the match."

He put the box on the bench beside me.

"Tell the boys their hot dogs are here," he said. Then he gave me a big smile and was gone.

The rest of my so-called team mates had started chanting in the showers.

"We're in the Final! We're in the Final," they kept repeating.

Thanks to *me* they were in the Final. And were they grateful? No, they were not

And could I have my own back on them and make them *very* sorry?

Yes, indeed I could.

I had given those zits to Pamela. OK, she had given them back to me. Still, it was me and my fossil who had wished them on her in the first place. I munched into one of Greasy Joe's hot dogs and tried to think.

What would I like to wish on my team mates?

They gave me the answer themselves.

"Can you think of anything more disgusting than Nick's zits?" one of them shouted.

"Nothing!" was Robbo's answer. "I'd rather have the runs for a week than zits like that."

The runs for a week?

I smiled to myself.

That could be arranged.

Chapter 5
The Runs

It was Monday morning and Robbo and the rest of the team were all in class. They looked fine. They didn't look pale. They didn't look sick. Had something gone wrong with my plan? Perhaps the fossil only worked once.

All through Anne-Marie's French lesson it was all I thought about. I had wished really hard, gripping the stone tightly in my hand all the time. So, why were they all at school this morning?

"Nicholas!" Anne-Marie shouted.
She always called me by my full name. "Pay some attention here! French is your worst subject and you have an exam in two weeks. Do you want to pass or not?"

Pamela leaned across and whispered. "She doesn't even know you're just as bad at English and maths."

I growled at her. "I'm going to try harder at French now, just so I can insult you in two languages."

She sniffed and turned away from me. She wasn't used to me insulting her like this. I was beginning to enjoy it.

Suddenly, Robbo got to his feet. He was pale and shaking and his voice sounded weak. "Please could I leave the ..."

He didn't wait for her answer. He was out of that class faster than you can say, 'The Runs'!

Anne-Marie called after him, but we could all hear Robbo's panicking footsteps pounding down the corridor. Our goalie got to his feet next. In a flash he was out of the class too. Next to go was our centre-half. Then our midfielder. One by one the whole football team went white as chalk and raced from the class.

The whole football team, that is, except me.

It was a wonderful feeling.

My spots were fading and I was having a brilliant revenge on my team mates.

I heard a mocking voice behind me. It was Pamela. "Why are you looking so happy?" she asked.

"Because I only have to look at your face. I don't have to wear it," I casually replied.

That threw her. She looked very surprised. Shocked even. She had always been so sure I really fancied her.

At geography the team still hadn't come back to class.

Ravi came running in, holding his nose. "I don't think we'll be able to use the boys' toilets for a few weeks."

By the end of the day most of the team had been sent home.

"The whole football team is ill," Goofy informed us. "I wonder why you're not ill too, Nick?"

I shrugged my shoulders. "Strange, isn't it?"

I strolled home, hands in my pockets, a happy chappy.

It was somewhere between the chemist's shop and the chippie that my stomach started making strange noises. I stopped dead. Suddenly, I felt as if my insides were being gripped and twisted in a hot vice.

I stopped strolling along.

I began to run. And I didn't stop running until I got home.

I only just made it in time.

I spent the next three days on the toilet.

I counted the fish on the wallpaper.

Six hundred and ninety three.

I counted every sheet on the toilet rolls.

NOT ENOUGH!!!

My whole family kept banging on the door.

"There's other people who need to get in there, you know," they yelled.

They even started visiting friends just to use their toilets.

When I got back to school on Monday, I discovered that the outbreak of the runs had been blamed on Greasy Joe's hot dogs.

"It was nothing to do with Greasy Joe's hot dogs!" I wanted to yell. "It was me. It was all thanks to me!"

But no-one would have listened or believed me.

It also turned out that I had had the runs worse than the rest of the team. They had all made it back to school on the Friday.

It was then I decided that I was doing something very wrong with that fossil. Every time I made a wish, I suffered more than anyone else.

The only member of the team who wasn't back at school was Robbo. His mother always spoiled him and she had decided that her "wee boy" needed a break. She had whisked him off for a holiday in Benidorm.

A holiday in Benidorm! I ask you. He was supposed to be suffering for what he did to me and instead he was sunning himself on a beach in Spain.

"That's where I'm going too," Ravi informed me.

"Really?" I said, not in the least bit interested.

"Yes. Remember that gold watch I found? Well, the man was so pleased with my honesty that he invited my whole family over to his villa in Spain."

This was getting worse by the minute. Why was nothing good happening to me!

I was getting very sick of this magic.

Everyone was in a terrible mood when I got back to school. It took me some time to

work out why. Then it hit me. I'd been so ill
that I'd forgotten the football final. It had
been that Saturday and the team, too weak to
play, had missed it.

"They should have put the match off till
later," I yelled at Big Gordy.

He shook his head. "That's not allowed in
an inter-school final. The other team turned
up. We didn't. So the match was theirs."

Without even kicking a football, the
trophy had gone to the other team.

The whole school was feeling fed up. And
I had never felt so guilty in all my life. I had
never meant this to happen. Why hadn't I
remembered the final? Whenever anyone at
school looked at me I was sure they could see
that it was all my fault. I had guilt written
all over my face.

"Don't look so worried, Nick," Ravi tried to make me feel better. "We're still in with a chance for the Schools' Quiz Final."

The Quiz Final. I had forgotten about that too. Maybe not so exciting as football, but a final just the same.

"Brilliant!" I said, feeling better already. "We're bound to win that. Robbo never gets a question wrong …"

Robbo! Suddenly, I remembered that Robbo, the star of the quiz team as well as the football team, was sunning himself on a beach in Benidorm.

"Is he coming back for it?" I grabbed at Ravi. "He has to come back for it."

Ravi pushed me away from him. "His mother won't let him. But it's not a problem. We're using the substitute."

The sub. And who was that?

Now I realised why the school was so gloomy. The light dawned on me. "You're the sub, Ravi."

He was almost bursting with pride. "That's right, I'm the sub," he said.

"You?" I was ready to cry. "That same Ravi who can't remember a thing when he's nervous? *That* Ravi is the sub for the Schools' Quiz Final?"

We were doomed.

Chapter 6
The Quiz Final

Ravi looked offended. "What do you mean that same Ravi who can't remember a thing when he's nervous? *That* Ravi ..."

"Well, let's face it, Ravi. The last time you were on the school's quiz team you lost us points because you couldn't remember your own name."

"It's going to be different this time. I'm using memory aids. I've got a book out of the library, *How To Improve Your Memory Overnight.* I won't let the school down."

A small crowd had gathered round him as he spoke. Not one of them believed him.

"You'll need more than memory aids to win, Ravi," someone said. "You'll need some magic."

Some magic. That was it. Magic.

Why not, I thought? If I could wish for something bad to happen, surely I could wish for something good too? The school needed to win this final. Because of me, we had lost our chance of the football trophy. Because of me, I decided, we were going to win the Quiz Final instead. I wanted to see some smiles on people's faces again.

That night I sat in my room with the fossil held tightly in my hand.

I chose my words carefully. This fossil was stupid. It never seemed to get things right. This time I wanted to get the message straight. This time nothing must go wrong.

"Let Ravi remember every answer in the school quiz," I said, very slowly. "I don't want him to be nervous. I just want us to win the Final. Right?"

I stared at the stone for a long time, daring it to answer me back. Surely, I thought, nothing could go wrong this time. I gripped the stone in my hand and it felt warm to the touch. This time, it just had to work.

On the night of the Quiz Final, I was the one who was nervous. I took a seat beside Goofy. He looked at me with concern.

"You still look pale, Nick. Are you sure you feel all right?" he asked.

"I feel sick," I nearly told him.

Ravi walked onto the stage with the rest of the team. No, in fact he tripped over his own feet and landed with a thud. The school let out a groan.

The other team looked more than confident. They looked smug. Everyone knew Ravi was hopeless at quizzes. They knew they were bound to win.

The quiz began. There was a hush in the hall. Each member of the teams answered their first questions correctly.

Then it was Ravi's turn.

"To which Royal House did Henry the Eighth belong?"

Ravi swallowed hard. He hesitated. I held my breath.

"Phone a friend," someone in the audience yelled at him.

"He won't have any friends by the time this is over."

Suddenly, Ravi sat up straight. He yelled back. "I don't have to phone a friend. I know the answer."

There was a gasp of disbelief from the audience.

Ravi stuck out his chest proudly. "The Royal House of Tudor is the answer." He said it with confidence.

He got it right.

We were all gobsmacked. We sat in stunned silence as he answered every single question after that like an expert. He was so calm about it. He sat back in his seat and studied his nails as he gave one correct answer after another.

There was one more question to go. If he knew the answer to this one, we had won. The trophy would be ours.

"What do they sell in Smithfield Market?"

This time, he hesitated. He bit his lip.
Then he turned to the audience with a
wide-eyed, puzzled frown. We all held our
breath.

Then Ravi, the little devil, beamed from
ear to ear. "Only kidding!" he shouted. Then
he barked out the answer with confidence.
"They sell meat in Smithfield Market."

A riot broke out in the hall. People
banged on the floor with their feet. School
ties and blazers were thrown in the air.
Ravi was carried shoulder-high from the hall
like a hero.

"Ravi's the Champion! Ravi's the
Champion!"

Everyone took up the chant.

"Ravi's the Champion!"

But *he* wasn't the hero of the day. Once
again, it was all thanks to me. This was hard

to take. *I* should have been the one carried shoulder-high out of the hall. Instead, I got no thanks at all.

However, it was worth it. The mood of the school changed completely. Everyone was happy. I even heard Goofy singing in his classroom. Either that or he was strangling a cat.

Even Anne-Marie was delighted. "This is such a happy school to work in," she said a couple of mornings later.

"And you know, Nicholas," she stopped at my desk and smiled at me. She is so pretty I grinned back like an idiot. "Ravi's brains must have rubbed off on you. You have passed your French exam, with, how do you say ... the flying colours?"

I had passed my French exam? And not only had I passed my French exam, but I passed my English and my maths exams too.

This was indeed a miracle.

No. It wasn't a miracle.

It was magic.

Chapter 7
Three Times Three

I thought about what had happened. And I saw that whenever I had made a wish for someone else, the wish had come true for me as well.

I had wished for zits on Pamela and what had I got?

More zits.

I had wished the football team to get the runs and what did I get? A triple dose of the runs too.

And look what happened with Ravi. I'd wished, really carefully, for him to know all the answers in the school quiz. And what had happened to me? I had passed all my exams. French. Maths. English. My worst subjects.

Then, I remembered that on the school outing when Ravi had first picked up the stone he had made a wish too. He had wished for poor old Goofy to find a stone. And he had.

But what had happened to Ravi?

He had discovered a gold watch. He'd got a £50 reward. His whole family had been invited to a villa in Spain. Good fortune had come to him three times over after he made that wish for Goofy.

Goofy. Why hadn't I thought of him before? He knew all about stones. He was the man to ask. He'd know if a stone could work magic.

I went to find him. He was sitting on the floor behind his desk. A shelf full of books had just fallen on him.

He didn't look very happy.

"It's just not my lucky day," he said as I helped him up.

I followed his miserable gaze towards the door where Anne-Marie was being chatted up by the new History teacher.

Gooty sucked at his teeth and shrugged his shoulders. "Lovely lady your French teacher. I'm not her type, of course. A pity."

At that point, I have to say, I wasn't very interested in his love life. "Can I ask you something about stones ... fossils?" I said.

His eyes lit up. Apart from Anne-Marie, stones were the only things he cared about.

"Yes, of course, but I didn't think stones were your thing, Nick."

"They're not, most of the time," I admitted. "But you told us on our day out that some old tribes thought they had magic in them. Remember? That day when Ravi found that funny looking stone and then lost it. Remember?"

"Every single stone has a history, Nick. Every last one of them. Just think how long they took to form. Think how many people have held them in their hands. Maybe some of these people who touched those stones left some of their own magic behind."

"Ah yes, *magic*," I said, pleased he'd mentioned it first. "Do you think they could make wishes come true?"

He peered at me. "Are you taking the mickey?"

I didn't want to annoy him so I said quickly, "No, Sir, honest. I was just thinking of a ..." I had to think fast. "A story for English, about an old fossil, like the one we found, that had been used by Celtic tribes to make their wishes come true."

Goofy's eyes lit up. He was really interested now. "That's what some tribes *did* believe, Nick. That a wish on certain fossil stones would come true. That would make a great story."

"Yes, but in my story, I was thinking that every time the handsome hero makes a wish for other people, something happens to him as well."

Goofy began to get really excited. "That's another old belief, Nick. What you wish for comes back to you. Three times three."

Three times three! If he'd hit me with a frying pan I couldn't have been more shocked.

The zits.

The runs.

The answers to the quiz.

I had got them all too – three times as bad or three times as good!

"Three times three," I repeated in a daze.

"The number three, Nick, has always been thought of as a magic number," Goofy went on. "Good luck and bad luck, all wrapped up in that number. Don't people always say that bad things happen three at a time? And good things too? In the Bible, Peter betrayed Jesus three times, didn't he? And we always say 'Three cheers', don't we? And what about third time lucky?" He patted me on the back. "That would make a very good story, Nick.

You must let me read it when you've finished."

Then Goofy looked out into the corridor again and my stone, my story and three times three were forgotten. They were pushed into the back of his mind by something more powerful than magic.

Love.

Anne-Marie was laughing. The new History teacher was looking pleased with himself. He was big, good-looking and had teeth that sparkled. Goofy didn't stand a chance against him.

It would take a miracle for the lovely Anne-Marie to even look his way.

A miracle, or a little bit of magic.

I closed my hand around the stone in my pocket and I shut out every other thought.

"Let Goofy have his Anne-Marie. She's everything he's ever dreamed of. Let him be everything she's ever dreamed of too. The love of both their lives."

I took a deep breath. I watched the teacher closely.

Anne-Marie was still laughing and Goofy was trying to pretend he wasn't watching her. He began to climb onto a shaky, old chair to put a great pile of books onto the top shelf.

"Why don't you just go out there and carry her off like a knight in shining armour?"

I didn't add that with Goofy's teeth he looked more like the knight's horse.

Goofy just gave me a sad, helpless look. I knew he'd never have the nerve to do anything like that.

He reached up towards the top shelf with the books. I walked off and began to wonder when my magic would start working.

I didn't have to wait very long.

There was a sudden strangled cry, followed by a crash and a thud.

I looked back quickly and Goofy had vanished under a fallen shelf, his pile of books and the old, broken chair.

The History teacher started to laugh. I was ready to join in, but Anne-Marie was furious.

"What do you think you are laughing at?" she demanded.

"He's an idiot. Always tripping over something," he said, "or something falls on top of him."

Anne-Marie lifted her pretty, little nose in the air. "He's worth three of you!" she snapped and then ran over to help Goofy. She threw herself on her knees beside Goofy. She pulled the shelf off his head. Then she hugged him close to her.

"Oh, Mr Dunn, are you all right?"

Was Goofy all right? I'd never seen a happier-looking horse!

Next day it was all round the school. Old Goofy and Anne-Marie had overnight become an 'item'. All thanks to me.

Of course, I couldn't tell anyone, could I? Who would believe me?

But I was waiting. Because if I was right ... and I knew I probably was right ... any minute now I would have every gorgeous-looking girl in the school kissing me.

When the bell rang for the end of school I was still waiting. I stood at the school gates and watched Goofy and Anne Marie walk hand in hand to his car.

Talk about an odd couple!

"Romantic, isn't it?"

I looked round to find Pamela standing beside me. She had a silly grin on her face. "You see, Nick, the ugly bloke *can* get a beautiful girl. There's hope for you yet."

I was about to say something back when Pamela did something really strange. She took out her lipstick and began putting it on those soft, full lips of hers. It was my favourite colour of lipstick too. The colour I told her she should wear. Purple.

"Pamela," I asked, "are you flirting with me?"

She let out a long, big sigh. "You *are* slow, Nick Black. You're as thick as you are ugly."

Then she started fixing her hair the way girls do when they want you to notice them.

"Is that your idea of telling me you fancy me?" I asked.

"Maybe," she said. But then, she did something even better. She leaned close to me and blew, ever so softly, right in my ear.

I felt the hairs on the back of my neck tingle. Wow!

"Well? Have I got to ask you to walk me home?" she said and gave my arm a tug. Pamela is not your shy kind of girl.

I had dreamed that every good-looking girl in the school would fancy me. But this, this was better than anything I could ever have wished for.

In fact, it was three times better.

Chapter 8
Giving Back the Fossil

It was time to give back the fossil. Something just told me that it was.

The next evening, I was going to meet Pamela at the coffee shop. Yes, we were now an 'item' too. On the way, I dropped in at Ravi's house. His Dad led me into Ravi's bedroom.

"Ravi spends all his time in here studying stones," he told me with a frown. "What did I ever do to get a son as daft as that?"

Mr Singh always dressed like Elvis Presley and spoke with an American accent. He'd a cheek to talk about Ravi being daft.

When I went into the room, Ravi was studying a long box filled with stones, pebbles and bits of rock. It took him a minute or two to notice I was there.

"Hi, Nick," he looked up, smiling. "Why are you here?"

I took the fossil out of my pocket and held it out to him. "I came to give you back this. It's yours. You found it. During the school outing, remember?"

He took it from me and turned it over once or twice in his hand. "Where did you find it?"

"I didn't find it, Ravi." I decided to be honest. "I stole it from you."

He didn't look surprised, or angry. He simply looked puzzled. "Why?" he said.

I shrugged my shoulders. "I don't know. You'd found lots of things. You'd found the gold watch. Perhaps I just wanted *something* to take home."

Suddenly, I knew that if I was going to be honest about one thing, I might as well be honest about the whole story. "No. That's not really true. I stole it because it was special."

Ravi nodded as if he understood. "I know, but they're all special, aren't they?" And he pointed to the stones in the box.

"No, Ravi, this one is really special. It's magic."

He looked puzzled again. "Magic?" he asked.

"It can make your wishes come true. Do you remember, Ravi, the day you found it and you wished that Goofy could find one too? And he did," I snapped my fingers, "just like that."

"Nick," Ravi spoke to me as if I was an idiot, "we were on a beach covered with stones. Of course he found one. He would have to be blind not to."

"But then, Ravi, right after that, you found the gold watch."

"That was just a bit of luck," he said.

"And you got a reward and you were invited to a villa in Spain. That's more than luck. That's magic."

He didn't agree with me. "That only proves that honesty pays off, Nick," he said smugly.

"Listen to this then. When I took the stone I made a wish too. I wished those zits on Pamela."

It took him five minutes to stop laughing. When he did he only said, "She used some new skin cream, Nick. That's what gave her zits."

"And then because I wished that, I got zits three times worse than hers."

Ravi was trying hard not to laugh again. He made me sit down. "Look, Nick. You got those zits because Pamela rubbed her face all over yours. Simple as that." He went slightly green at the thought of it.

I shook my head. "No, Ravi, it was magic!"

"Rubbish!" he said.

I carried on, determined to make him believe me. "I gave the whole football team the runs."

He didn't hesitate. "That was Greasy Joe's hot dogs."

"I got them worse than anybody else."

"You ate two."

He had an answer to everything.

"OK, then. How do you think you knew all the answers in the school quiz? I wished for that."

This time he didn't look puzzled. He looked angry. "Wait a minute, Nick. I stayed up all night studying for that school quiz. I had a book out of the library, *How To Improve Your Memory Overnight*. Don't you dare take the credit for that."

I didn't argue with him about that one. "But," I said, "how come I passed in my three worst subjects? And I didn't read your book! Don't you see what's happening here? Everything I wish for comes back to me, three times three!"

I refused to give up. He had to understand the power of that fossil stone. "It's thanks to me that Goofy finally got his Anne-Marie."

Even he, I thought, couldn't explain that one.

But he did.

"Anne-Marie's fancied Goofy for ages. She's just been waiting for him to make a move. Didn't you notice that she was always giggling with the other teachers whenever Goofy was around? She was trying to make him notice her. It was only a matter of time before they got together."

I couldn't believe it. "I never knew that."

Ravi was shaking his head. "That's because you're not a man of the world like me, Nick."

"Well, you can't say Pamela's always been trying to make me notice her. She's always hated me. And now she's my girlfriend. I wished for Anne-Marie and Goofy to get together and I got the wish back three times better. I got Pamela."

Sometimes I really hate the way Ravi talks down to me. As if I was very, very stupid. It was like that now.

"Nick, son," he placed a hand on my shoulder, "Pamela couldn't stand you because you were wet. You blushed and talked rubbish whenever she was about. But as soon as you played hard to get and started insulting her, she was hooked. Women are like that. You know the old saying? Treat them mean, keep them keen."

"You've got an answer for everything, Ravi. But I'm telling you. There's magic in that fossil. Tribal magic."

"You're the type who'd believe anything, Nick," he said and held the fossil out to me. "Look at it. It's only an old stone."

"It's going to be wasted on you, Ravi."

I almost asked him to give it back to me, but before I could open my mouth he had dropped it in the box with all the other stones. Hundreds of them. I couldn't have picked it out again if I tried.

"See," he said, "they're all the same, except to experts like me. To me, they're all special."

"Rubbish!" I told him.

As he led me to his front door he put a hand on my shoulder. "You've just learned an important lesson, my son." He was getting up my nose talking to me like my old uncle. "You only get out of this world what you put into it. Three times three."

But I didn't believe him. That old fossil was magic.

I'll always believe that.

Barrington Stoke would like to thank all its readers for commenting on the manuscript before publication and in particular:

Eileen Armstrong
Anthea Beale
Liam Bird
Ann Bradfield
Mandy Jane Cambray
Matthew Cleevely
Jamie Costello
Jack Dailly
Lee Derby
Luke Douglas
Vivian Faichney
Robert Ferguson
Kelly Field
Clinton Fitch
John Garty
June Hawkings
Caroline Holden
Nancy Hunter
Mark Jarman
Valerie Johnson

Mark Lilburn
Linda McDougall
Jason Mackenzie
Amanda Minns
Donna Murray
Dean Newman
Cheryleigh Niven
Stephanie Pears
Jason Tomson Pottinger
Aimee Richards
Mark Richards
Nadeem Rubbani
Mark Sanderson
James Saunders
Michelle Scott
Stacey Shields
Ryan Stevens
Gemma Thompson
Amanda Tye
Matthew Wiley

Become a Consultant!

Would you like to give us feedback on our titles before they are published? Contact us at the email address below – we'd love to hear from you!

Email: info@barringtonstoke.co.uk
www.barringtonstoke.co.uk

If you ~~loved this~~ book, why

Hi Lo

don't you read ...

Sticks and Stones
by Catherine MacPhail

ISBN 1-842992-95-3

Greg's sure he's the funniest and most popular guy in school. So why does everybody think he's stolen Tony Harris' mobile phone? But it can't be a set-up. After all, everbody loves him ... don't they? He's going to need all his brains, and some help, to get him out of this one!

You can order *Sticks and Stones* directly from our website at **www.barringtonstoke.co.uk**